For Angi

Marley & Florence

The Great King's Treasure

Marley and Florence were best friends.

The best friends anyone in the whole world could be.

They went everywhere together, had the best adventures and even had tea parties with Florence's dolls.

But there was a secret that only Florence knew.

Marley was no ordinary dog. Marley was special.

Not just special because Mum and Dad thought he was.

Not just special because he wore an eye patch like a pirate.

He was extra special. Marley could talk.

"Let's go and play with the teddies, Florence," said Marley once Mum had left the room.

"We can't today Marley, we have a very important mission to do!", replied Florence, already packing her backpack.

"Another mission? What adventure are we having today?" Asked Marley excitedly, wagging his little tail as fast as a helicopter propeller.

"Today Marley, we are going on a hunt to find The Great King's Treasure! Legend has it that it's lost in the depths of the wild jungle," replied Florence.

"How exciting! I'll get my teddy!" Shouted Marley, running upstairs to fetch his favourite toy.

Ready for their mission, the pair set off…..to the back garden.

Dad hadn't cut the grass in so long that it had grown to be taller than Marley and Florence, which was great for them as they had the most amazing adventures, pretending the grass was a maze, a forest and today a jungle.

"Be brave Marley, there are wild animals in here, but it will be worth it when we find the treasure" said Florence, using her doll to hit the grass out of their way.

"I'm always brave! Brave is my middle name." Said Marley, knowing full well his middle name was not Brave.

They went deeper and deeper into the jungle, until they could hardly see the back of the house.

"A SNAKE!" Shouted Florence in alarm.

Marley quickly jumped in front of Florence, "Marley Power!" He bellowed with a loud woof, dragging the garden hose out of their path.

"That was a close one Marley, let's carry on to The Great King's Castle." instructed Florence.

Finally, they reached Florence's sand pit at the edge of the garden.

"I know The Great King's Treasure is around here somewhere, use your Super Smell, Marley," said Florence, hoping his nose was as good as he says.

Marley put his nose to the ground and sniffed like he'd never sniffed before.

"I've found something!" exclaimed Marley, very proud of himself.

They started digging through the sand with their hands and paws until there was no sand left in the pit.

They had found it.

A beautiful, golden bone tag with The Great King's name on it.

"Quick Marley, let's show mum what we found!" said Florence eagerly.

They ran back through the long grass as quick as their little legs could go.

Mum was in the kitchen preparing lunch when Florence and Marley burst through the back door.

"Mum! Mum! We have something to show you!" panted Florence out of breath.

Marley dropped the golden tag into mum's hand.

Mum's eyes went wide.

"Oh, you two, where did you find this? I thought it was lost forever!" Said mum with tears in her eyes.

"In the jungle," replied Florence, grinning at Marley, "I told you it would be worth it, Marley, it's the treasure you lost mum."

"A treasure it certainly is," said mum, "let's put it with his photo."

Mum missed her old dog, Winston, very much. He lost his tag in the garden a long time ago, before Florence was even born! Mum had never been able to find it. But Florence knew she and Marley would. They were the best treasure hunters there ever was.

Sat at the table eating lunch, Marley watched his teddy go round and round in the washing machine. It had gotten rather dirty on their adventure.

Mum had put the special treasure next to Winston's photo in the living room. Pride of place for The Great King.

Mum sat down with them to eat her sandwich, "Well I hope you've enjoyed your wonderful adventures in the garden Florence, your dad is cutting the grass tomorrow."

"NOOOOO!!" Screamed Florence, making Marley jump, "he can't!"

"Why ever not?" asked mum.

Florence looked at Marley with a knowing grin. Marley smiled.

"Because tomorrow, we're going dinosaur hunting!"

More from C.M. Bennici

Billy's Bubblegum
Freddie's Fishy Pet
Jack in the Box
Scarlett and the Unicorn

www.cmbennici.com

Printed in Great Britain
by Amazon